Albert's Ballgame

written & illustrated by
Leslie Tryon

ALADDIN PAPERBACKS

Special thanks to Patrick Lyon
1994 Carmel Valley Little League All Stars

First Aladdin Paperbacks edition March 1999

Copyright © 1996 by Leslie Tryon

Aladdin Paperbacks
An imprint of Simon & Schuster
Children's Publishing Division
1230 Avenue of the Americas
New York, NY 10020

Also available in an Atheneum Books for Young Readers hardcover edition.
Book design by Becky Terhune
The text of this book is set in Pike.
The illustrations are rendered in gouache.

Printed in Hong Kong
10 9 8 7 6 5 4 3 2 1

The Library of Congress has cataloged the hardcover edition as follows:
Tryon, Leslie.
Albert's Ballgame / written and illustrated by Leslie Tryon. — 1st ed.
p.   cm.
Summary: As springtime comes to Pleasant Valley, everyone who is anyone,
which means of course everyone, plays ball.
ISBN: 0-689-80187-4
[1. Baseball—Fiction.   2. Ducks—Fiction.   3. Animals—Fiction.]
I. Title.
PZ7.T7865Pl   1996
[Fic]—dc20   95-15300
ISBN 0-689-82349-5 (Aladdin pbk.)

For Con Pederson
Pleasant Valley's Commissioner of Baseball

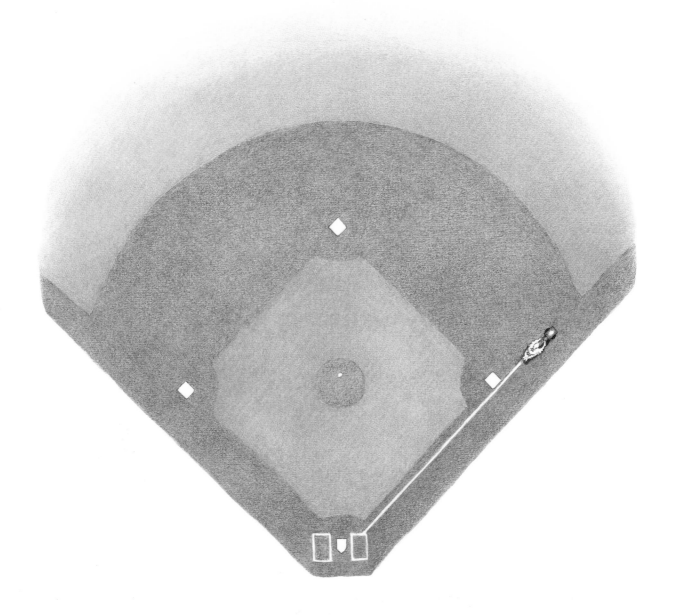

Picture books
by Leslie Tryon

When it's springtime
in Pleasant Valley,

Everyone who

is anyone . . .

Which means of course everyone in Pleasant Valley...

Goes to the Old Field.

Why does everyone who is anyone, which means of course everyone, go to the Old Field?

Because when it's springtime in Pleasant Valley, it's time to…

PLAY
BALL!

They
pitch
beanballs

and
mean
balls,

knuckleballs,

and
chuckleballs.

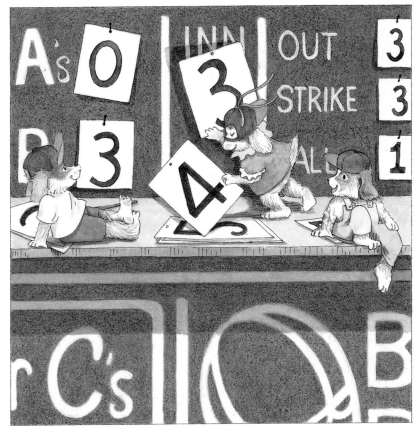

They pitch
balls…

"Hey, that was inside!"

They hit
fly balls

and
sky balls,

slow balls,

and
toe balls.

They hit foul balls way back
or too wide.

They shag
horn balls
and
corn balls,

sticky balls and
licky balls.

They tag beach balls that ride

on the tide.

They catch
stray balls
and spray balls,
curve balls
and swerve balls.

And they
miss balls
if they
should collide.

They stride home
and glide home.
They walk, steal,
and slide home.
They might even
hit a

HOME RUN!

They will pitch, hit, and run.
They will catch and have fun.
For this is just the beginning.

One team has lost, the other has won.
In the fall we will see who is winning.

Pleasant Valley Ducks

Manager: Albert

Position	A's	B's
1 Pitcher	Jim – Squirrel	Howler – Monkey
2 Catcher	Willie – Kangaroo	Patrick – Monkey
3 1st base	Georgie – Cat	David – Ostrich
4 2nd base	Mair – Otter	Pat – Raccoon
5 3rd base	Adam – Rabbit	Lacey – Ostrich
6 Shortstop	Frog	Sandy – Pig
7 Left Field	Tapper – Monkey	Jo – Mouse
8 Center Field	Judy – Ostrich	Ashley – Ostrich
9 Right Field	Kathy – Hedgehog	Gracie – Cat

Home Umpire – Sir Cedric
Bat Rabbit – Justin